HOW NIGHT CAME TO BE

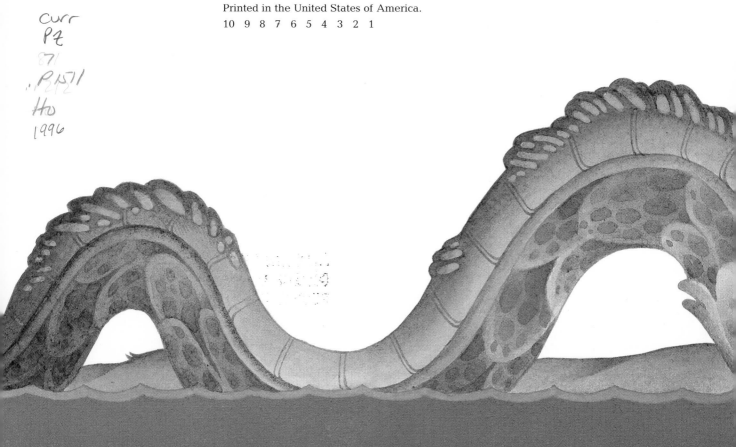

First-Start® Legends

HOW NIGHT CAME TO BE

A STORY FROM BRAZIL

Retold by Janet Palazzo-Craig
Illustrated by Felipe Davalos

Troll

Long ago, there was no night.
Daylight filled the sky.

Darkness could be found in only one place—under the sea. A great Sea Serpent ruled the ocean. He lived there with his daughter. Her name was Bonita.

One day, Bonita left her dark home. She saw the beauty of the land. Off she walked into the jungle.

Soon Bonita came to a village. The people had never seen such a beautiful girl. Their chief fell in love with her at once.

"Please stay with us," he said.

Bonita stayed. In time, the two married.

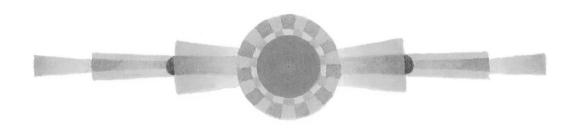

They lived happily. But after some time, Bonita grew sad. "What is wrong?" asked the chief.

"I love the light of this world," said Bonita. "But I miss the darkness. I am tired and want to rest my eyes."

The chief told three men to go to the Sea Serpent. "Ask him for some darkness so Bonita may rest."

The men went to the sea. They asked the Sea Serpent for a bit of darkness.

The Sea Serpent put some darkness into a bag. He rose above the water. "Here is darkness for my daughter," he roared. "Do not open this bag!"

The three men took the bag and hurried away.

At first, all went well. Then the men heard strange sounds. Squealing, screeching sounds came from the bag!

The men were afraid. "What shall we do?" they asked.

"Let us run away!" said one.

"No," said the second man. "Let us sit on the bag. Maybe then it will be quiet."

The third man said, "Let us open the bag."

"No!" cried the others. But it was too late. The third man had opened the bag. Out flew darkness and the creatures of the night. The men ran!

Bonita saw the darkness. "At last, night has come!" she said. She closed her eyes and slept.

The next morning, Bonita awoke. She heard the birds singing. She saw the morning light. "What beautiful songs the birds sing," she said. "They greet the new day."

When the three men told the chief that they had disobeyed the Sea Serpent, he grew angry. "I shall change you into monkeys. Go live in the trees!"

And that is exactly what happened.

Bonita picked up the empty bag from her father. Inside was a white shell. She threw it into the sky. It became the moon!

Now we have darkness and light each day. Birds sing each morning to greet the day. Each evening, the night creatures come out.

And always, we can look at the moon and remember the Sea Serpent and his gift of darkness.

How Night Came to Be is a legend from Brazil. Legends that tell how something came to be are often called *myths*. People from many different lands have myths to explain the daily passage from daylight to darkness.

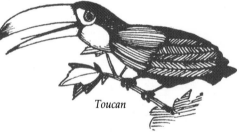

Toucan